T0419559

NORMAL KIDS

NORMAL KIDS

Melinda Di Lorenzo

orca soundings

ORCA BOOK PUBLISHERS

Published in Canada and the United States in 2024 by Orca Book Publishers.
orcabook.com

Library and Archives Canada Cataloguing in Publication
Title: Normal kids / Melinda Di Lorenzo.
Names: Di Lorenzo, Melinda, 1977- author.
Series: Orca soundings.
Description: Series statement: Orca soundings
Identifiers: Canadiana (print) 20230473210 | Canadiana (ebook) 20230473229 |
ISBN 9781459838574 (softcover) | ISBN 9781459838581 (PDF) |
ISBN 9781459838598 (EPUB)
Subjects: LCGFT: Novels.
Classification: LCC PS8607.I23 N67 2024 | DDC jC813/.6—dc23

Library of Congress Control Number: 2023942160

Summary: In this high-interest accessible novel for teen readers, Hannah goes on a search for her younger brother, who has disappeared with their overdue rent money, and finds unexpected romance along the way.

Orca Book Publishers is committed to reducing the consumption of nonrenewable resources in the production of our books. We make every effort to use materials that support a sustainable future.

Orca Book Publishers gratefully acknowledges the support for its publishing programs provided by the following agencies: the Government of Canada, the Canada Council for the Arts and the Province of British Columbia through the BC Arts Council and the Book Publishing Tax Credit.

Design by Ella Collier
Edited by Doeun Rivendell
Cover photography by Shutterstock.com/Stock Holm

Print and bound in Canada.

27 26 25 24 • 1 2 3 4

Chapter One

The first thing I see is an empty vodka bottle. The glass is on its side. It sits on the tile floor in the entryway, and the red label is like a warning. My heart drops.

"Mom?" I call.

I don't expect an answer, and I don't get one. I step inside and close the door behind me. I make my way to the living room. My heart drops even more.

In the ten hours since I left for my shift at Ye Olde Pizza, a mess has formed. Food cartons fill the coffee table. An overflowing ashtray sits there too. There's even broken glass on the carpet. How it happened, I don't know.

That's not quite true, I think. *I know a little bit.*

When my mom drinks, she spreads chaos everywhere.

"Mom?" I say again.

I put my hands on my hips. Another thing that happens when she's drinking is that *I* become the parent. It sucks. Especially because my younger brother, Seth, is a pain in the ass. He's fourteen, and I'm seventeen. He doesn't respect me. Not that he respects anyone. But Seth is a lot like our mom. And unlike in some families, that isn't a compliment. Party now. Say sorry later.

I step over a pile of clothes and a man's work boot, and I shake my head.

"Gross," I say.

But I keep moving. I have no choice. I have to go to my mom's room. On my way out this morning, our landlord stopped me in the hall and told me our rent is overdue. Based on what I see now, I can't imagine my mom followed through. And we *have* to pay.

Mom's last bender almost got us kicked out. The one before that got her locked up for thirty days. Seth and I spent three months in the shittiest foster house in the world. That's where his problems started. I never want to go through that again.

I knock on Mom's door. "Are you in there?"

I hear a noise, so I push the handle a little. Her room is worse than the rest of the apartment.

Her laundry is piling up, and it's starting to smell. The window is open, even though it's been raining and windy. The floor has a big dark spot on it, and I'm not sure if it's water or something worse. There are a lot of other things spread around too, but I don't look closely at any of them. The truth is, I don't want to know.

I step in. Then I wish I hadn't. My mom is lying on the bed. Her too-skinny legs are sticking out from a ratty old blanket. And a big man I've never seen before is butt naked beside her.

"Jesus." I cover my eyes and raise my voice. "Mom!"

The man groans, and I silently beg him not to wake up. The boyfriends Mom picks when she's on a bender are always awful. Low-life scumbags.

"Mom?" I say. "Please wake up."

After a long second she finally speaks. "Hannah? S'that you?"

Her words are slurred. I can tell she's still wasted. I want to get out of the room. Fast. But I need to pay the rent.

"Gary needs the money, Mom," I say. "Did you forget?"

She pauses so long that I think she's passed out again. But right when I'm about to yell her name, she answers me.

"Didn't forget," she says. "Gave the money to Seth."

"Seth?" I repeat.

She laughs like I've said something funny. "Your brother, silly."

I press my teeth together. "Yeah. Thanks. I got that."

I spin on my heel. She says something else as I leave, but I ignore her. I hurry to the room I share with Seth.

"Hey," I say toward the curtain that divides the space down the middle. "Did you give the money to Gary? It's the third month we've been late."

There's no answer. A common theme in my house, I guess.

"Hey!" I'm annoyed now. "Seth."

When he still doesn't answer, I grab the curtain and pull it back. My brother's area is empty. Or at least empty of *him*. It's full of other stuff, though. It reminds me of Mom's room, which is depressing.

For a second I just stare at it. Like I can't help myself.

We have a rule that we don't go into each other's space. Of course, Seth has to walk through my side to get to his. But I can't remember the last time I looked on the other side of the curtain. His area is full. Really, really full.

A desk I've never seen before is squished between the bed and the wall. A stack of old CDs sits on top of it. So does a disc player that was my mom's back in the day. Random bits of paper are everywhere. A pile of porn mags is right in the middle of the tiny bit of floor. I glare at those for a second, grossed out but unable to look away at the same time.

"Really?" I say to my missing brother. "You couldn't even hide them somewhere?"

Then I look around a bit more. Seth has about ten weird-looking plants on a shelf. Beside those are too many collectible action figures to count.

I make a face and turn to the bed. That's where Seth usually hangs out. Attached to his headphones and listening to hip-hop. Probably stoned about 80 percent of the time. Today the sheets are bunched up, and a bong rests on his pillow.

"Really?" I say again.

I roll my eyes, and I step past the curtain. My plan is to move the drug stuff out of sight. But when I get closer to the bed, I see something that makes my blood run cold and fast at the same time.

Under the bong is a torn envelope. The word *RENT* is written across the top. And the envelope is empty. Which is bad. But what's worse is that Seth's cell phone is lying beside it. My brother would never leave his phone behind on purpose. Not in a million years.

Chapter Two

"Shit, shit, shit," I say.

My heart thuds a little too hard in my chest, and I hurry over to grab the phone. Things don't get any better when I pick it up. The screen is a cracked mess.

Okay, I say to myself. *The phone is garbage, and that's probably why he didn't take it.*

I want it to make me feel better, but it doesn't. Yeah, I'm a little less worried. My pulse drops to a reasonable level. But now I'm more pissed off too. Not only does Seth have our goddamn rent money, but I have no way to get a hold of him. On top of that, when this is over I'll have to find some way to get him a new phone. God knows our mom won't do it.

I tap the screen, just in case. The only thing that happens is a piece of glass falls off. It plinks onto the ground then disappears under the bed. The phone stays black. I can't even see his ridiculous screen saver, which is his elbow, bent to look like a hairy ass crack. Classy all the way. That's my brother.

"If you aren't already dead, I'll kill you myself," I mutter.

As soon as the words are out, I regret them. They sound bad, and the room is too quiet without Seth in it. He's not dead, though. I feel like I would know if he was. But he's probably in some kind of trouble. Because he's *always* in some kind of trouble.

Uneasily I eye the phone again. Did my brother get mad and break it? He makes some shitty choices, but he's usually chill to the point that it annoys me. Nothing bothers him. I can't picture him getting mad enough to smash his phone. Of the two of us, I'm the one more likely to explode. Right now my fingers are itching to become a fist. Frustration presses down on my shoulders.

Most of the time, I do okay with extra responsibility. Cooking dinner? Sure. Tossing out my mom's beer cans? Fine. I don't even mind forging her signature on school paperwork. But shit like this isn't supposed to be my problem. I'm not even in twelfth grade yet. It's summer. I'm seventeen. I should be worrying about what to wear to the beach and what song to listen to on my way there.

"But no," I say under my breath. "I have to pay the rent and make sure my mom isn't sleeping in her own puke. Good times."

I force my hand open and toss my brother's phone onto his bed.

Okay, Hannah. What would a normal kid do in this situation?

It sounds like a silly question, I know. Obviously I'm not a total freak. But "Normal Kid" is a game Seth and I made up when we were a lot younger. If our mom was doing her thing, and it got messy, we'd pretend to live in some big house somewhere else. A place with a pool and a dishwasher, mostly.

What would a normal kid do? I'd ask my brother.

And he'd say, *I dunno. Eat popcorn,* or another little-kid thing like that.

I get a weird squeeze in my chest thinking about it now. We haven't played the game in a gazillion years. We barely look at each other now. If we're in the same room, it's because he's done something shitty, and I have to fix it.

But what *would* a normal kid do if her brother took off like this?

I answer myself out loud. "Tell her parents."

For obvious reasons, my mom is a bad choice. And Seth and I have different dads, and neither of them is around. Mine abandoned our mom when she was pregnant with me. Seth's dad left when he was two.

Some normal kids might call the cops if their parents weren't around as well. Also not an option for me. They know Seth by sight, and my mom's been in lockup a few times too. Cops plus the Dresher family never equals anything good.

I have to look for him myself. Sooner rather than later.

"Great. Just great."

I let out a groan and abandon Seth's half of the room and move back into mine. Quickly I strip out of my Ye Olde Pizza uniform—which I think looks like a pirate costume, by the way—and put on regular clothes. My favorite jeans with the rips in the knees.

A vintage rock-concert T-shirt I stole from my mom's closet years ago. The black lace-up boots I bought with my tips. When I'm done, I force my long, curly hair into a bun and take a look in the mirror.

My blond roots are starting to show from under the red dye. My black eye makeup is a bit smudged. But I'm on a mission to stop my family from getting kicked out of our apartment, not trying to impress anyone.

"Okay, Hannah," I say to my reflection. "Get it done."

I'm about to yell to my mom that I'm going out when she yells at me instead.

"Could you two brats keep it down out there?" she calls. "Some of us are trying to sleep."

I roll my eyes. I don't know what she thinks she heard, but it sure as hell wasn't me or my brother.

"And since when are we young enough to be called *brats* anyway?" I say under my breath.

But I don't bother to answer my mom. I walk quietly through the apartment, into the entryway, and slide out the front door.

In hopes of avoiding our landlord, I take the back stairs instead of the elevator. And in under a minute, I'm out on our street in the warm August-evening air.

For a second I feel free. It's like that a lot when I leave the apartment. Fresh air. Not so much pressure. But tonight it lasts for less than a heartbeat. I picture Seth's broken phone, and the good feeling goes away. I *have* to get that rent back. I can't stand the thought of what will happen if I don't, and I shiver even though it's not cold.

I walk without thinking about it. Kind of aimlessly. I don't even realize where I'm headed until I'm practically right in front of the sign.

Welcome to Sandy Beaches!

Well, that's what it used to say. But someone has spray-painted over the words. Now it says something else.

Welcome, Salty Bitches!

I'd laugh, but I'm too worried about getting the hell out of there before someone sees me.

Sandy Beaches is the absolute worst part of town. And that's saying something, coming from me.

There are no beaches. Nothing sandy nearby. If someone's in the mood to get a knife held to their throat for pocket change, this is a damn fine place for it. But for some reason, my feet stay where they are.

Why did I come here? Do I seriously think Seth might be in Sandy Beaches?

I chew on the inside of my lip for a second. God knows this is a place where my brother could score some decent dope. Especially with our rent money.

I shake my head and start to turn back. But I barely move before a hand lands on my shoulder.

Chapter Three

Thank God my reaction is too slow and kind of weak sauce. If I'd moved quicker, I would've accidentally kicked a cop in the balls. Because that's who's standing behind me. He's dressed in the standard blue uniform, and he's got sharp blue eyes and an intense stare. I want to drop my gaze even though I'm not guilty of anything.

"Do I know you?" he asks.

"I don't think so," I reply, praying that he's not one of the cops who's picked up my mom for something.

"I think I do know you." His stare gets even sharper. "You work at the pizza place."

My shoulders sag a bit, and I pull out some extra politeness. "Yes, sir. I'm a server."

"Had a pepperoni-and-mushroom there last week. Delicious." He pauses. "You live around here?"

I shake my head. "No, sir."

"You know where you are then?" he asks.

I resist an urge to point at the *Sandy Beaches/Salty Bitches* sign.

"Just out for a walk," I say.

He studies me like he's looking for a lie. I keep my chin up until he finally nods.

"No crime in a walk," he tells me. "But you might want to steer clear of the yellow house around the corner. Unless you're looking for something pretty hard-core, that is."

He tips me an expectant look. Does he really think I'd admit it if I were here to buy drugs?

I shake my head. "No, sir. Just getting some fresh air."

"All right," he says. "My advice is to think about clearing out before it gets dark. Sun goes down, and every shitrat in the neighborhood comes out. Air stops being fresh, if you catch my drift."

"Thanks."

Now I really do turn and walk away from Sandy Beaches. But I'm not aimless anymore. The cop's comments about the drug house gave me an idea.

There's this sketchy dude, Quincy, who sells bad weed outside a corner store across the street from our school. Seth definitely buys off him. And chances are pretty good that my brother would hit up a trusted source before going anywhere else.

I walk fast, and I'm not gonna lie, it's good to have a destination. My feet tap the sidewalk in a steady rhythm. In my head I imagine finding my brother with Quincy. I'll give him shit. Not too much in front of the sketchy drug dealer. Seth will already be embarrassed and pissed off. I don't want to ruin his life, even though he's constantly screwing up mine. But I want him to know he can't do stuff like this.

Hopefully he hasn't spent too much of the money, I think. *And hopefully I made enough tips today to cover whatever he* did *spend.*

It takes about twenty minutes, but I finally get to the school. No more cops stop me, thankfully. But when I walk over to the corner store, I run into a different problem. There's a sign on the door that says the owner is on vacation.

No customers for Quincy the dope dealer.

"Sucks to be you, Quincy," I mutter.

It'd be funny if it weren't for the fact that it means Seth's not there either.

"Dammit, Seth," I say. "Where are you? What am I supposed to—"

I cut myself off because I'm not alone. There's a boy about my age standing at the other end of the parking lot, and he's staring at me so hard that I take a step back.

"Can I *help* you?" I ask.

He clearly doesn't pick up on my sarcasm. Actually, he seems to think it's an invitation, and he comes closer.

"Do I know you?" he asks, just like the cop did.

But I don't bother with the extra politeness with this guy. "I dunno. Do you?"

Yeah, yeah. It sounds super immature.

But he just gets even closer, looking at me with a pair of really dark brown eyes that match his really dark brown hair.

He's got to be a foot taller than I am, so over six feet for sure. He's got narrow shoulders, but he's not really skinny. Just…*long*. Long arms. Long legs. Long chest. I'd bet my life that people ask him all the time if he plays basketball. I want to blurt out the question myself even though I don't care about basketball at all.

Think maybe it's because he's kinda hot? asks a little voice in my head.

I'm suddenly glad that I'm not prone to blushing. Because the voice is right. He's got a nice jaw that's not perfect and thick eyebrows that make his eyes look even darker. The only reason I didn't notice before is that he startled me.

"I *do* know you," he says after another second.

"Let me guess," I reply, "you ordered a pepperoni-and-mushroom last week too."

His forehead creases into a frown. "What?"

I sigh. "Never mind. It was awesome not really meeting you, but I've got to go."

"Wait."

I don't know why I listen—maybe the hotness again—but I do.

"Math class," he says.

Now *I* frown. Wouldn't I have noticed someone like him in one of my classes? Cute. Tall. And now that I'm looking at him more closely…dressed pretty nicely too. Black cargo pants that haven't faded. A collared black shirt, flecked with crimson splotches that almost look like fake blood. And a pair of new-looking Chucks.

"I joined late, and I sat in the back," he tells me. "I always do. People can't see over my head. And for some reason, no one in the front ever turns around."

It's a fair point. I don't think I've ever looked at the back even once. Mostly because I'm trying to pay attention. I have to work my ass off in math to pull a decent mark.

"Makes sense," I say. "But I've still gotta go."

"I suck at math," he adds.

"Sorry to hear that. Bye now." I give a little wave and turn to leave.

"Wait," he says for the second time.

"Dude. I've seriously loved this chat, but I've got a family thing."

I'm going to keep walking, I swear. But then he says something that makes me stay again. And this time it's got nothing to do with his hotness at all.

"You're looking for Seth Dresher? I think I can help you."

Chapter Four

Even though it's still warm out, goose bumps rise up over my body. Someone can be both hot and creepy. I've seen enough serial-killer documentaries to know. But I order myself not to freak out, and I narrow my eyes at the boy who knows my brother's name.

"How the hell do you know that?" I ask. "And what makes you think I want help from some weirdo I just met in the street?"

"A weirdo who's bad at math," he corrects with a flash of very even, very white teeth.

I will 100 percent *not* be charmed. I cross my arms over my chest and give him my best don't-fuck-with-me glare.

"You've got about ten seconds to explain," I tell him.

He puts his hands up in mock surrender. "I said I was bad at math, but I'm pretty damn good at putting two and two together."

"If you think you're being clever, you're not. Five seconds now."

"Okay, okay." He draws a breath, then lets out an extra-long sentence. "I heard you say out loud that you wondered where Seth is, and you said it was a family thing, and I suddenly remembered your last name from math class."

I relax a tiny bit. "Fine. But why does that mean *you* can help me?"

"Because in a super-weird coincidence, I heard

some guy talking about him today," he says. "Some jerk over at Smith's. You know the place, right?"

I relax even more, and I nod. Everyone in town knows Smith's. It's an arcade that's got a reputation for serving drinks to minors. Seth definitely hangs out there. I've heard him mention it.

"What did the guy say?" I ask.

He shrugs. "Just that some kid named Seth Dresher owed some punks some cash."

My heart rate gets faster. It's a good explanation for why my brother took the rent money. I mean, not *good* good. But something that fits.

"What punks?" I want to know.

The tall dude shifts from one foot to the other, looking uncomfortable.

"You might as well just tell me," I say. "I'll figure it out anyway. It'll just take longer, and my brother will be in even more trouble."

Shit. I hadn't meant to say the last bit. But the guy doesn't comment on it, thank God.

"If I tell you where I think they are, will you let me come with you?" he asks.

I should say no. I don't need some kid from my school getting into my private family life. I keep even my friends far away from it. But I remember what the cop said about the "shitrats" coming out at night. The sun is starting to go down. And I'm not even close to being a chicken, but I can think of worse things than not being alone in some bad place. Which is undoubtedly where I'll find my brother.

I nod. "Okay. You can come with me. But for the record, I don't need a bodyguard."

"I'd settle for being a sidekick," the boy says.

I will *not* smile. "I don't need one of those either."

"I'm Eli, by the way."

"Hannah. But I guess you know that."

"Yeah." He grabs the back of his neck in a sheepish way. "I do."

Did he know it all along? I kind of think he did, and it gives me a funny feeling in my chest. A nice feeling.

Oh, good, I think. *Now I like being stalked.*

My face feels warm even though I'm *really* not a blusher. I cover my awkwardness by lifting one of my eyebrows.

"So?" I say.

"Right," Eli replies. "The guy talking about your brother mentioned Pine Ridge. Something about that big brick apartment building there?"

Great.

It's another run-down community. I mean, it's not quite as overrun with shady-ass people like Sandy Beaches. But still.

Goddamn Seth and his goddamn problems.

I couldn't be angrier at my brother if I tried.

Gritting my teeth, I start walking without waiting for Eli and without saying anything. Of course, he catches up after I've taken only three steps. His long legs make it easy for him. He walks right beside me, and I expect him to ask questions. Or at least to make useless small talk. But he's totally silent, and I swear almost ten minutes go by. Once, his hand brushes mine, and I have to pretend that it doesn't make my skin tingle. It's me who finally speaks first.

"So, uh, did you fail math?" I ask.

"I passed," he says. "Barely. What about you?"

I got an A, but only because of how hard I worked. But telling him that seems like a humble brag, so I just shrug.

"I did okay," I state.

"I bet you aced it. I never heard you get an answer wrong."

"Maybe I *stole* the answers. Ever think of that?"

He laughs, and it's that kind of laugh that makes other people want to join in. Hell, *I* want to, but I don't let myself. There's no reason to let him know that I like it. I stare straight ahead instead, pressing my lips together until the urge passes. Another minute or two go by, and Eli still doesn't say anything else.

I purse my lips. Is it weird that he's not being curious?

"What were you doing out by the school?" I ask after some more long silence.

"Definitely not drawing a picture of a giant dick on Mrs. Stubb's door," Eli replies.

I almost trip over my feet. "What?"

"I said that's *not* what I was doing."

"Dude."

He laughs again, and this time I can't stop myself from joining in. I have no idea if he was really adding some questionable art to the school. But the thought of it is pretty damn funny. Particularly since Mrs. Stubb is the hard-ass principal who no one likes. But as funny as it is, my amusement wears off quickly. We're almost at Pine Ridge. I can already see the gray apartment building, and I don't like how intimidating it looks.

"Still want to keep going?" Eli asks.

I realize I've unconsciously slowed down. Now I consciously speed up without answering him. He doesn't ask again, and pretty quickly we get to the front of the building. But that's about it. The second we reach the walkway that leads to the door, my spine goes cold. I look up. Right away I spot a big dude on a third-floor balcony. He's so enormous that he seems to take up the whole space. I swear he has something gun-shaped tucked into his waistband. And he's looking right at us.

Chapter Five

My blood pumps through my body so hard that I can hear it in my head. *Whoosh, whoosh,* it goes, making me feel kind of sick. There's not much that really scares me, but guns totally freak me out.

So much for Pine Ridge not being as bad as Sandy Beaches.

I don't realize I'm stuck to the spot until Eli's hand finds mine. He gives me a tug. Not hard. But enough to bring me back to life. My feet start working again. I squeeze his fingers tightly until we go around the next corner. Even then, I kinda wish I could keep holding on without it being weird. I make myself let go.

"You okay?" Eli asks.

"What the hell was that about?" My question comes out sounding shaky, but I don't care if he notices or not. I'm just worried about my brother.

Eli shakes his head. "Dunno. Did you recognize that guy?"

"No." Now my voice is smaller than I want it to be.

Seth, what did you get yourself into?

"He looked like a bouncer at a club or something," Eli adds.

More like an enforcer for a gang, I think.

Which could be what he is for real. And I have exactly zero doubts that if Seth *is* somewhere in the building, it's the same place as the wannabe bouncer.

I want to let out a frustrated scream. *Goddamn Seth and his goddamn problems. Again.* I've somehow gone from looking for my brother to maybe getting on the bad side of a guy with a gun.

"You okay?" Eli asks again.

My shoulders feel heavy. I have an unexpected urge to tell him everything. About Seth. About my mom. Even about some of the other shit in my life in general that led up to today's glorious failure. But my brain tells me it would be entirely unreasonable. I don't know Eli, and I sure as hell don't trust people I don't know. Not even when they're nice and cute and looking at me all worried.

"I'm fine," I lie. "Just thinking. I need to figure out a way to get in there without that guy seeing me."

"Maybe there's a back way in," Eli says. "Like an alley for the garbage guys or something."

"Genius," I reply, meaning it.

Eli looks so pleased that I don't even bother to protest when he leads the way. I just follow him around the other end of the block. And sure enough, there it is—a narrow space between two rows of buildings.

"Double genius," I say.

I move closer, and the smell of rotting garbage slides up my nose. I fight a gag. Eli seems less bothered by the stench.

"At least we know no one will be hanging out back here," he says.

A rat goes scurrying by. I don't tell Eli I've seen people spending time in equally gross places, and I look around. My eyes land on a row of ladders. Fire escapes, actually.

Perfect.

Stepping wide around a pile of discarded clothes, I make my way to the nearest ladder. I peer up. It looks like it goes to an emergency exit rather than to an actual apartment. But of course I can't reach the ladder. And of course Eli can. Before I even ask, he extends his arms up and grabs the bottom rung.

I hold my breath, waiting for the screech of scraping metal. When it doesn't come, I almost laugh. It's like someone came back here and greased up the ladder for us. It makes only the lightest thump when its legs hit the ground.

Eli gestures toward it. "Not sure if it's more sexist to say 'ladies first' or offer to go first myself, so…"

"Bold of you to assume the choice between the two is yours," I reply.

I slide past him, put my hands on the sides of the ladder, then start climbing. I get to the third floor quickly, and I pull myself onto the platform and wait. Eli gets up fast too, and in seconds he's beside me. With him there, the platform is a lot smaller. It's not built for two. We can't move without bumping each other, and Eli says "Sorry" twice before he gives up and goes still. We stand that way for a long moment. I can smell whatever deodorant or cologne he's wearing. It's sweet and tangy, and a hell of a lot better than the garbage smell below us. I inhale, then glance at Eli, hoping he hasn't noticed what I just did. But his eyes aren't on me. They're on the metal door that's blocking our way.

"How are we going to get in?" he asks in a low voice.

"Amateur," I whisper back.

I yank my wallet from my pocket and pull out my movie points card. I bend down, put one hand on the doorknob and slide the card in just above the lock. It takes some focus, but I get it done. The lock clicks open, and I twist the handle.

"Should I be impressed or scared?" Eli asks.

"Yes," I joke.

Slowly I lean my shoulder into the door and push it open. I peer inside. There's no one to see. But a thumping beat carries into the hallway, and the heavy scent of weed keeps the music company. Still cautious, I step into the hallway, then suck in a breath. The second door on our left is wide open. It has to be where we need to go. I'm about to tell Eli, but I don't get a chance to speak. Because right then the bouncer slash gang enforcer with the gun steps out of the apartment.

Chapter Six

"How the hell did you little shits get in here?" the big guy asks.

And he really *is* big. Taller than Eli. Half as wide as the hallway. His head seems to almost touch the ceiling, and his scar-shredded face couldn't be less pleasant if it tried. Like he read a how-to book on being a criminal. But it's the metal sticking out of his waistband that freezes me. Only my brain works.

Dammit, Hannah, it says to me. *Answer him.*

But my tongue is gummy. It refuses to make words, and my eyes won't leave the gun. But luckily Eli isn't affected like me. And clearly I've forgotten about not wanting a bodyguard because I let him step in front of me to answer for us.

"How about we tell you how we got in, and you let us talk to your boss in exchange?" he replies. "Good to know if there's a security risk, right?"

The response I expect to hear from the bouncer dude is, *How about you just tell me, and I won't shoot out your kneecaps?*

Instead someone inside the apartment hollers, "Christ, Jones. Let 'em in. See what they want."

Jones looks anything but pleased. But at least he waves us forward.

"Don't touch anything, dipshits," he says.

Eli leans a little closer and speaks right into my ear. "Didn't know we were headed into a museum. Maybe it's full of retro hash pipes or something?"

Despite my fear, a laugh bubbles up. I swipe my hand over my mouth to keep it from coming out.

"If that *is* what's in there," Eli adds, "I am most definitely touching things."

Now I have to cover a laugh with a cough.

"Weirdo," I whisper as we step into the apartment.

There's no entryway. It just opens right into a living room that's packed with people. Three girls about my age are sharing an armchair. A dude in his twenties sits with his legs hanging off a stool, and five people are crammed onto a loveseat. A few more hang around, seemingly oblivious of the lack of space and the cloud of smoke. But the ones who stand out are a guy and a girl on a full couch. They have three times as much room as anyone else, and my eyes focus on them.

The girl is uninteresting. Very pretty. Long blond hair. A lot of makeup. Tight black crop top and cut-off shorts. She's spinning some plastic toy in her hand. She must've graduated already, but she looks like half the girls at my school. The guy is different. He's for sure the oldest person in the room. He's gotta be thirty. He's got a scruffy beard and tiny round glasses, and a mess of dark, curly hair. A tattoo pokes out from under his shirt collar. But I don't dare look at it long enough to figure out what it is. Too much attention would be a death wish or something.

At least he doesn't have a gun. I pause. *Not that you can see anyway, Hannah.*

Watching us, he takes a drag from the joint in his hand. He holds in the smoke for so long that I'm surprised he doesn't choke. Even when he lets it out, there isn't a hint of a cough.

"I hear you went to a lot of trouble to get in here," Tattooed Old Guy states.

My tongue has gone back to being all weird. But Eli touches my back for a heartbeat, then drops his hand and answers for me.

"We came up the fire escape," he says. "We're looking for Seth Dresher."

"Why?" Tattooed Old Guy replies.

I finally find my voice, and it's at least a little bit firm. "He's my brother, and he owes me money."

He leans back and tosses an arm over the shoulders of Crop Top Girl. "Well, that I can relate to."

Please don't let Seth have given him our rent money, I think. *Because no way in hell is this guy going to give it back.*

"Lotta people owe me money a lotta the time," Tattooed Old Guy adds. "Not your bro. Not this week."

I'm relieved and disappointed at the same time. I don't want Seth to have given our money to this dude. But now I'm back to having no clue where my brother has gone.

Crop Top Girl stops spinning the thing in her hand.

"Wait," she says. "Is Seth the kid with the thing right here?"

She points to her left cheek.

His birthmark.

It's a small but noticeable pink splotch right where the girl has her finger.

I nod and don't bother to hide my eagerness. "Yeah, that's him."

"Oh, that kid was around this morning," she says.

"Was he now?" replies Tattooed Old Guy.

The girl rolls her eyes. "Don't be jealous. It was before you got up."

"I'm always up when you're around, baby," he says, grabbing his crotch.

Gross.

Eli clears his throat. "Any idea where he might've gone?"

"Dunno," the girl says. "Maybe to that forest party that's happening tonight? He might've said something about it. I can't remember."

"What forest party?" Eli asks.

But I already know. I probably should've thought of it, actually. There's a couple of big clearings in the woods on the edge of town. A ton of kids party there every weekend. And no matter how many times the cops break it up, they keep going back.

"Thanks," I say. "We'll check it out."

The girl shrugs. "Hope you get your money back. Brothers suck."

Without thinking about it, I grab Eli's hand again. All I want is to get out of there and to do it fast. But Tattooed Old Guy calls out as we turn around.

"Hey!" he says.

My shoulders tighten. I should pretend I didn't hear him, but I can't quite do it. I look back.

"Go out the front door," Tattooed Old Guy tells me. "You wouldn't want to get hurt *by accident*."

The way he says "by accident" makes me think he means the opposite. The gun flashes into my mind, and I really have to force myself to nod. Then I squeeze Eli's hand even tighter and practically yank him from the apartment. I can't get outside fast enough. But when we get to the main floor and burst through the doors, I stop cold and suck in a startled breath. It's gotten a lot darker while we were in the apartment. And the night feels like a weighted blanket in a bad way.

Shit. Time is passing too fast.

"You okay?" Eli asks.

It's the third time he's posed that exact question. And it's the second time I've wanted to confess the truth about what's going on.

No, I'm not okay, I want to say. *If I don't find out where the hell Seth is, I'll be packing my bags yet again. And who knows what shithole we'll wind up in this time?*

My throat gets scratchy. God, how I want to say it all. But Eli is still just some guy I don't know. One who hasn't even asked me for any details. And what I really need to do is get him to leave so I can get on with my own stuff.

I pull my hand out of his and pretend it didn't feel better to be holding it.

"Look," I say, "your help was awesome. I literally wouldn't have gotten this far without you. But I'm good from here."

"I don't mind sticking around," Eli replies.

"Yeah, I get it. I'm just better on my own."

He looks at me like he wants to argue. His mouth kind of puckers, and his eyes narrow just the slightest bit. And he *does* speak. But what he says isn't at all what I expected to hear.

"One thing before I go," he says.

"Sure," I reply. "What?"

"Can I kiss you?"

Chapter Seven

Here is a list of things I should say in response to
Eli's question:

You can't be serious.

No.

Fuck off.

Fuck off twice.

What?

I don't have time for this.

Or maybe all six rolled into one.

Except that's not what I do. Instead I take a small step closer to him and nod. My body tingles. Almost vibrates.

I can have this one small thing, can't I?

Eli bends down and brushes his lips against mine. And even though I'm expecting the kiss, it still startles me. My eyes open wide. I'm stiff. It's like being struck by lightning or something. A head-to-toe shock. Then my eyelids flutter and sink shut, and I sink right along with them.

Eli's mouth is warm. Firm. The kiss takes up all the space in my head so that I can't even think about my brother anymore.

It's just Eli and me. And when his hand comes up, and his fingers find the back of my neck, I get dizzy and breathless. Can someone faint from being kissed like this? I want to cling to him. Maybe I *am* clinging to him. Because as he pulls his mouth back from mine, I realize my arms are around his waist. I have to force myself to let him go.

The world comes back into focus.

A siren sounds from somewhere nearby, as if to prove the moment is over.

"Thanks," Eli says, sounding all gruff and pleased.

"Uh, you're welcome?" I reply.

"I've been wanting to do that since the first second I saw you."

"You have?"

He flashes a grin. "Yep. Dream realized. See you around, Hannah. And good luck."

He shoves his hands in his pockets and turns away. My chest deflates. He's seriously leaving? Now?

He keeps walking without looking back.

You're disappointed, Hannah? You legit asked him to go.

"He respected your boundaries," I mutter to myself.

Yeah, after he kissed you.

"With your permission," I say under my breath.

I keep watching Eli. He's almost at the other end of the block already.

"Dude, what is *wrong* with you?" I ask myself.

My brain is hollering at me. And even though it should be telling me to hurry up and find Seth and our rent money, it's not. What it's telling me is that I should yell for Eli to come back. But it's unreasonable. And selfish. I have to get to the forest party. Get the money. *Not* get kicked out of our apartment. Kissing some boy isn't important compared to those things.

I almost win the argument with myself. I turn in the opposite direction. But at the last second, I pause and fling a look over my shoulder. If I'm being honest, I'm really just hoping that Eli will be looking at me too. He's not.

Asshole, I think, but I don't mean it.

I narrow my eyes. And before I can turn away again, I spot a group of kids heading Eli's way. Based on their size, I'd say they're a few years younger than us. There are six of them. I know right away that they're going to jump him. They're all in hoodies, and all the hoods are pulled up tight even though it's still warm. Two of the kids are looking back and forth, taking quick, nervous glances. *Boneheads.* All of them are clearly in need of a lesson on how *not* to look heaty.

My mouth opens, but I snap it shut again as a surge of hot anger slides through me. It's like lava bubbling under the surface.

I'm pissed off at Seth for stealing the money and generally being a douchey little brother. At least for the last year or more.

I'm angry with my mom for all her ongoing shit.

I'm mad at myself for who knows what reason.

I'm even annoyed at Eli for listening to me when I asked him to leave.

It all wants to burst to the surface. I stride forward, not caring what happens.

"Hey, dickheads!" I yell. "Ready to get your asses kicked by a girl?"

Every single one of them freezes. Six hooded faces turn my way. Eli's looking at me too, but I focus on the other kids. I recognize one of them from school. He's a ninth grader. It takes me only a second to remember his name.

"Walter Rippleton," I call out as I get closer.

The boy jerks like I've slapped him.

"That's right," I say. "I know who you are. And I'm in a shitty enough mood that I'll narc on you if I have to."

"Is she serious?" mutters one of the kids.

"Better yet," I add, "I'll just get my phone and film you. So go ahead. Go back to whatever you were about to do. Get ready to go viral."

It's an embarrassing threat, but it seems to work.

"What the actual fuck, lady," says another of the kids.

Lady. Ha.

I just glare in his direction. "Bet I could figure out who you are too. Wanna take the risk?"

"C'mon, man." It's a third kid speaking this time. "Let's get out of here."

"Good choice," I tell him.

I probably sound like a superhero talking to a villain in an action movie, but I don't care. The little punks scatter. I watch them go, my anger burning off as they disappear.

Eli, who's been silent this whole time, clears his throat.

"Again..." he says. "Not sure if I should be impressed or scared."

"I saved you from being jumped by peons," I reply. "Just be thankful you didn't have to swat them off like flies."

"Thanks."

"You're welcome."

It's nearly the same conversation we had right after we kissed, and warmth creeps along my skin.

"Do you still want me to leave?" Eli asks.

"Yes," I say quickly.

He tilts his head, then shrugs. "Okay."

I realize he's really going to take off again. More important, I realize I don't want him to.

"Wait," I say. "No."

"No, what?" he replies.

It takes some effort to admit it aloud, and I have to swallow a big lump in my throat. "I want you to come with me."

I'm tense after I say it. I've given myself a pretty damn good chance of getting made fun of. But Eli doesn't tease me.

"Good," he states. "I want to come too."

My whole body heaves a relieved sigh.

"Should we go now?" he asks.

I nod. "It's not that long of a walk. But just one thing before we leave."

"What?"

"Are you going to kiss me again?"

I'm joking. Kidding him. Trying to make it light so it's not awkward. But he looks at me with a dead-serious expression.

"The very second I can," he says.

Chapter Eight

I start walking, fast. My face is hot. And no matter how sure I am that I'm not a blusher, I'm pretty damn certain my cheeks are pink.

Eli's words bounce around in my head. *The very second I can.* He wants to kiss me again. He wants to do it soon. Do *I* want the same thing?

Yeah, of course you do.

It's the best kiss I've ever had. Probably because the only other kisses I've had were from playing Spin the Bottle at a party last year. No one there touched my cheek like some hero in one of those nineties rom-com movies that my mom loves.

But Eli did.

I steal a glance at him from the corner of my eye. I'm on the sidewalk, but he's on the road, and it makes us the tiniest bit closer in height. I have a better view of his face. He has some stubble on his jaw. Not the wispy kind that most guys my age get. It's thicker. Like he might really have to shave every day to stop himself from getting a beard. I have an urge to touch it to find out what it feels like. My hand even lifts up a little before I shove it back down at my side.

I am *not* a girl who gets all soft and whatever because some hot guy is paying attention to me. But at least it's a distraction from thinking about

Seth and the goddamn money. I'll have to focus on that again sooner than I want to.

"Were you actually in my math class last year?" I blurt.

Eli gives me a funny look. "Yeah. Why?"

Because it seems impossible that I wouldn't have noticed a guy like you, I think.

But I force out a different statement. "I just thought you might be lying."

"That'd be a weird thing to lie about," he replies.

"Yeah, well—" I cut myself off when his hand grabs mine.

A zap runs up my arm.

"I wouldn't lie to you," Eli says. "Ask me anything."

"I could ask you anything, and your answer might be a lie," I reply. "I have no way of knowing."

"Fair point."

We walk in silence for a minute or so. It seems strange and not strange at the same time. Here I am, holding hands with a dude I barely know. One who kissed me. Who I kissed back. A guy who's helping me look for my brother for no reason other than maybe he thinks I'm cute too.

"I hate having help," I say after another second.

Eli lets out one of his nice laughs. "Why?"

I hesitate. I argue with myself. Should I tell him personal things? I keep reminding myself that I don't know him. But how can I *get* to know him if I stay totally quiet? And it's not like he's pressed me for information. Maybe that's why I want to talk to him. No pressure.

"People can't be relied on," I tell him.

"Not all people," Eli says. "But some."

"But when you're let down a hundred times, it doesn't seem worth it to try for a hundred and one, right?" I reply.

"What if one hundred and one is the magic number?" he counters.

"There's no such thing as magic."

"Isn't there?"

He's teasing me. Being charming and cute. And I can admit it works enough to make me want to smile. But I'm not living a fairy tale.

"My life is shit, Eli," I say bluntly. "My mom drinks most of the time. My brother is a stoner thief who doesn't think about anyone but himself. I live in a garbage apartment in a garbage neighborhood."

"So?" Eli replies.

I'm kind of glad he doesn't argue with me. I don't want him to care about the sad parts of my life. But he's not getting it. Not really. Maybe I'm not giving him something hard enough. Something that makes him see I'm not some chick who gets a nice highlight reel like this. Late-summer fling? Hell no. Not for Hannah Dresher.

I pull my hand free even though I'd rather not.

"Back at that apartment, the guy with the gun freaked me out," I say.

"Freaked me out too," Eli agrees.

"But with me, it's just because of the gun," I reply. "And before you say that they scare lots of people, it's just vague fear for them, okay? The way they're scared of clowns or the dark. It's not real. For me, it's real. So listen for a sec, okay?" I look straight ahead as I talk. "When I was seven and my brother was five, my mom had this boyfriend…"

I explain it and relive it at the same time.

The boyfriend's name was Felix. He was twice my mom's age, and I can still picture him perfectly. Big, bushy beard. Bald head. Mean eyes. He liked to smack my mom. And even though I was pretty little, I'd never been so glad that Mom went through guys quickly. I couldn't wait for him to leave. Except Felix stuck around longer than most of her boyfriends did.

They were screaming at each other one night, and I couldn't find Seth. We usually hid together when shit got out of control. We lived in a small house back then. I tore through it looking for him. Felix and my mom kept going at it.

I finally hid under the couch, and Felix chased Mom into the living room. He had something in his hand. A gun. He was pointing it at my mom. Threatening her. She was daring him to shoot her. Calling him a coward. So he aimed it across the room and fired into this pile of clothes there. It was so loud. My body was frozen. My ears had that feeling like when you're underwater.

"And then the pile of clothes *moved*," I tell Eli. "It was Seth. He'd hidden under them. Just pure luck that the bullet missed him. Hashtag 'blessed,' right?"

"Jesus," Eli says.

I look at him. His nice eyes are wide. Yeah, now he gets it a little better. But he needs to get it even more.

"You'd think my mom would've kicked Felix out then," I say. "But nope. He stuck around for another three months. Left when *he* wanted to. Good times."

Now Eli doesn't say anything. I'm guessing he's shocked. Wondering why no one called social services or whatever. But that's just too bad, so sad for him. Eli can leave anytime. He can forget all about this and move on. Because Felix won't stay in his head the way he does in mine.

A few more silent seconds pass. We leave the paved street and cut onto a gravel path. Trees spring up in front of us, and we'll be in the forest soon. But before we get all the way there, two guys our age come stumbling out. They're yelling the lyrics to some classic rock song and passing a bottle back and forth between them. They pause when they get close enough to see us.

"Yo!" says the taller of the two. "You're totally Seth's sister, aren't you?"

My heart skips a beat, but I answer carefully. "I totally am. Why? Have you seen him?"

"Sick," says the short guy. "Yeah, we saw him. And bro was on *fire* earlier tonight. Hooking up with the hottest chick at the party in the park."

The two of them laugh, then high-five each other.

I grit my teeth. My brother making out with someone is *not* the visual I needed.

"How long ago did you see him?" I ask.

"Dunno," says the short one. "Couple of hours?"

"More like one hour," the tall one tells me. "Remember when Mohinder yelled that it was beer thirty?"

"Yeah, man," his buddy says. "Fuckin' hilarious."

One hour. Seth was here that *recently.*

"Probably still there," the short guy adds. "I mean, let's be real. I sure as hell wouldn't leave that girl."

"Damn, son," says his tall friend.

They high-five again, but now I really don't care. I'm already moving toward the forest.

Chapter Nine

Once we're in the woods, it's not hard to figure out which direction to go. It'd be harder *not* to figure it out actually. Hip-hop blares. Kids scream over top of the music. The bonfire smell seeps into the air too.

"Do they *want* to get caught?" Eli asks as we get closer to the noise.

I snort. "They don't care. It's like five minutes of intense fun, then someone yells, 'Cops!' and everyone runs for their lives."

We go around a bend and come face-to-face with two guys in a drunken wrestling match. One of them is wearing a horse mask. The other is in a skin-tight green suit. And they're clearly doing whatever the hell they're doing for their own entertainment, because they don't even have an audience.

"What the hell?" Eli says.

I meet his startled look with a raised eyebrow. "Are you sure you're a teenager?"

"I'm starting to question it," he replies.

"Says the guy who was *not* drawing penis graffiti at school earlier."

He grins in that charming way of his, and we step wide around the two guys and keep going. The music gets louder. I know the song that's playing, and now the kids' screams become distinct enough to understand.

Please let Seth be here.

Ahead of us the trees part. It's the exact kind of chaos I'd expect.

A bonfire burns in the middle of the clearing. Three topless dudes are running around the fire in a circle. Someone has built a tower out of inflatable pool toys, and a group of kids are throwing rocks at it. Across the field a bunch of people are using pieces of cardboard to slide down a grassy hill.

Where are you, Seth?

"There's a shit ton of people here," Eli says after a second. "See your brother anywhere?"

I shake my head. There are way too many kids to make it an easy search. And Seth's the kind of guy who blends in anyway. He likes plain black T-shirts and jeans, and he's got brown hair that he keeps cut short. He could be anywhere in the crowd, and I might not spot him.

"Guess I'll just look for the prettiest girl here instead," I mutter.

Eli catches my eye, and I shake my head again, this time for a different reason.

"Don't you dare," I tell him.

The side of his mouth twitches. "I have no idea what you're talking about."

I glare. I know he was going to say that *I'm* the prettiest girl here. I'm 100 percent certain of it. But I can't make the accusation unless he admits it. And now that he knows *I* know...no way is he going to admit it.

"Fine," I say with an eye roll. "Let's imagine what those two shitheads back there would classify as hot. My suggestion is that we just look for the chick with the biggest—"

I cut myself off as a girl with waist-length red hair catches my attention. She's tall and slim and curvy at the same time. She's wearing a pink dress that catches the light from the bonfire. Anyone would notice her. Right now at least three slobbering assholes are staring at her. And I'd bet whatever's left of the rent money she's the hot chick my brother was with. Well, maybe not the *rent money*. Because I really do want that back. But I'd bet a body part or something.

"Come on," I say to Eli. "That's gotta be her."

"How do you know?" he replies.

I turn to roll my eyes at him a second time, but he looks genuinely puzzled. His eyebrows are scrunched together in a frown.

"You can't possibly think she's not hot," I say.

He shrugs. "Not my type."

"Well, trust me," I say. "It's her. Let's go."

We walk over to the redhead, who's even prettier up close. But her greenish eyes are cold, and I have to dig down and find some niceness.

"Excuse me," I say. "I'm looking for my brother. I heard you guys were hanging out tonight."

"Sorry," the girl replies. "Wrong person."

She turns away from me, and I grind my teeth together. I haven't told her my brother's name. Or even said what he looks like. How would she know I have the wrong person?

Liar, I think.

I raise my voice. "We just need to find him."

She turns back with a sigh. "Didn't you hear what I just said? You. Have. The. Wrong. Person."

Eli touches my elbow. A warning. I glance past the redhead and see a guy in a hockey jersey watching us from a few feet away. He looks far too interested. And he's got a half-crushed beer can in his hand. As I watch, he lifts the beer and chugs it. Then he lets out a belch and tosses the can to the ground. And he stomps on it. Because of course he does. But I can't just let it go. Seth and the money matter more than some drunk asshole.

"Please," I say to the girl.

"I'm with someone else," she replies. "I don't know Seth like that."

We both freeze. She said his name. The name I haven't said.

"Please," I say. "If you have *any* idea where he might be, tell me."

Her face goes flat. "You're making a mistake, and you need to back the fuck off. If you don't, my boyfriend will kick your boyfriend's ass."

I blink. My *boyfriend*? What does she mean? *Shit.* She's talking about Eli. I'm distracted for a second. He's not my boyfriend. Not even close.

But what would it be like if he was?

"I'm not kidding," the girl says.

C'mon, Hannah. Keep your shit together. Seth and the money. Focus.

"Look. I only care about—" I stop talking when I see that the guy in the hockey jersey is moving closer to us.

His hand is in a fist. Dammit. No way am I going to let Eli get into a fight for my sake. I'd rather take on the other boy myself. But whatever shit is about to start is cut short by some kid's yell.

"Cops!"

I couldn't have predicted it better if I tried. And everyone, us included, books it.

Chapter Ten

Branches and bushes bite my skin. My legs burn. So do my lungs. It's dark and impossible to see where we're headed. But Eli's hand never leaves mine. He holds on tight, and once, when I trip, he keeps me on my feet.

Soon the sound of other kids freaking out fades. The trees get thinner. Streetlights become visible between the bits of brown and green, and we slow down a little. When we get to the very edge of the woods, I tug Eli to a stop.

I'm breathing so hard that I'm wheezing. I sound like a guy my mom dated once. He smoked three packs of cigarettes a day, and every time he laughed, it turned into a cough. But at least Eli isn't doing any better than I am. He's got a hand on a wide tree trunk, holding himself up. And he's clearly in need of a rest as much as I am.

"Next time you want to run a marathon, give me some warning so I can get some stretches in first," he gasps.

"Guess you don't play basketball after all," I reply in an equally breathless voice.

He sucks in another big breath and expels it in a heave. "What?"

I wave my hand. "Nothing. Never mind."

"Think I pulled a calf muscle," he says.

"Welcome to my world. We only run when the cops are chasing us."

"Ha."

Eli shifts so that his back is against the tree, and he closes his eyes. I stay where I am for a minute, watching him recover. For some reason, I'm surprised that he didn't use this as a chance to get away from me. He could've easily lost me in the woods. Let my hand go. Perfect excuse for a clean escape. Or clean-*ish* anyway.

Didn't the story about the gun scare the shit out of him? Kiss or no kiss, why is he still here?

"You okay?" he asks when he opens his eyes and catches me staring.

I look down at my feet and clear my throat. "Yeah. I'm fine. Except I still don't know what the hell to do about my brother."

Unexpectedly, Eli reaches out and pulls me into his chest. He smells nice. Like the cologne or whatever I smelled when we were on the fire escape. I let myself enjoy it for a second before sighing.

"I'm running out of places to look," I say into his shirt.

"So stop looking," Eli replies.

I lean back and stare up at him. "I can't do that."

"He'll turn up eventually."

"It's not that simple."

Eli kisses my forehead, then my cheek. My breath catches.

"Then *make* it simple," he says. "Get him to pay you back tomorrow. Then we can go do something else."

He kisses my other cheek, then my nose. And God, it's cheesily romantic. And I don't have time for cheese or romance. But that doesn't make me pull away. If anything, I lean in even more. Eli's hands slide down my forearms, and he threads his fingers through mine. I tip my head up.

"I mean, don't get me wrong," he says. "This is still a hell of a lot better than what I'm supposed to be doing."

His lips are so close now that I can feel them vibrating.

"What are you supposed to be doing?" I ask.

"Working for my dad," he replies.

"Oh yeah?" I'm only talking because I like the rumble of his words against my mouth, and I don't want it to stop. "Doing what?"

"Stuff."

"Stuff?" I echo.

He doesn't answer. Instead he brings his hand to my cheek. He kisses my lips lightly, three times in a row, before letting me go and easing away. I hate the sudden space between us.

"Seriously," he says. "Let's do something else."

"I really can't, Eli."

"Why not?"

I hesitate.

How is telling him the truth about why you need the money any worse than telling him the gun story?

It's probably not. But Felix is in my past. The current situation is my reality. It's my humiliation. And even though I'm used to it, and don't give all that many shits what people think, this is different somehow. I meet his eyes. He's frowning, and his gaze is worried. Why does it feel so wrong to keep the truth a secret?

C'mon, Hannah. Give him a bit of trust.

"It's our rent money," I explain. "If I don't get it to him today, our landlord will kick us out. My mom is wasted at the moment. In bed with some asshole. So it has to be me."

"How much is it?" he asks.

"Twelve hundred bucks."

"Maybe I can help you."

I make a face. "How? Have you got a wad of hundreds in your pocket or something?"

He grabs the back of his neck with his hand. It's the same thing he did when he admitted to knowing my name before I told him.

He legit might have the cash.

"Are you serious right now?" I say.

He reaches into his cargo pocket and yanks out an envelope. A hundred-dollar bill peeks out from the top. And there are more under it.

I can't take it from him. Of course I can't. But hope bubbles anyway.

"Where did you get that much money?" I ask.

"Does it matter?" Eli replies.

An uneasy feeling threads its way along my shoulders.

"Of course it matters," I say. "If you're a thief or a drug dealer, you should just tell me now."

I'm being sarcastic, but it crosses my mind that it might actually be true. My throat tightens.

Don't let it be true.

Eli shifts from foot to foot, visibly uncomfortable. "It's my dad's money. From the apartments and whatever."

"What?"

"The rent he collects. That I collect for him."

It takes me a ridiculously long second to catch on.

Duh, Hannah. He's rich. His family owns apartments like yours. And he thinks that's going to bother you.

And the bad thing is, it does.

Eli keeps talking. Assuring me everything he's said to me tonight is true. He just left out some details. Like the fact that his parents own four buildings. *Four!* Two are in an area I passed through, which is where he first spotted me before following me to the corner store. Explaining that his parents own the goddamn arcade where he heard the guys talking about my brother.

I hear it, but I don't care. I'm so pissed off that a fire burns in my chest. I can practically taste the sparks of it. He said he wouldn't lie to me, but he did. Leaving something out is the same thing. Like when my mom says she's going out with a friend. But then forgets to mention that she's planning on spending the whole night doing vodka shots.

How could I have let him fool me like this? I know better.

I don't even realize I've spun and started to walk away until Eli calls out.

"Hey!" he says. "Where are you going?"

"Some of us have things to do." I snap the reply over my shoulder.

"Hey!" Eli calls again. "Hannah!"

But his voice is getting farther behind me. And this time, I'm pretty sure he won't follow me.

Chapter Eleven

My feet thud slowly against the pavement, and the sound is dull and slow.

Thump.

Thump.

Thump.

Thump.

The noise matches the pathetic beats of my heart.

Five minutes ago I was kissing a guy I thought was funny and cute and on my side. I mean, things weren't perfect right then either. I still hadn't known where to find Seth, just like now. But at least I'd had help. Fast-forward to this moment, and I'm right back at the beginning. I'm alone. Pretty much clueless about where to look for my brother. And to add to that bullshit, there's a thick, scratchy feeling in my throat. The kind I get when I'm sick. Or when I'm about to cry. And I can't remember the last time I did the second thing. Stuff sucks so often that there's no point in drowning in it. But I know I'm not sick.

So what does that tell you, Hannah?

"Shut up," I whisper to myself. "You don't know what you're talking about."

But my brain doesn't listen to my voice. It keeps churning out my mistakes and tossing them back at me.

You've spent the whole night with Eli, chasing down a measly few bucks so you don't get kicked out of your apartment. And it backfired. In fact, he might as well be the one kicking you out. His parents own buildings just like the one where you live. And Eli knew it all along too.

I argue with myself. The last part of my thoughts isn't quite true. He didn't know about the overdue rent. And as far as I can tell, he's not an asshole at all.

"Or maybe I just don't *want* him to be an asshole," I say.

Okay, that might be the truth. Especially since I told him about my mom and Felix. Nobody wants an asshole knowing their secrets.

I sigh. I want to look over my shoulder to see if I'm wrong about him not following me. I make my eyes stay forward. But I don't have the same control over my ears or feet, apparently. My walk slows down.

The thumping eases to a tap. And I strain for some sound that Eli is behind me. There's nothing.

My shoulders droop. I kick a rock out of my way, then wince when my toe stings.

"Seriously. What's your deal right now, Hannah?" I mutter.

But maybe I know the answer. Maybe the problem is me and my fucking pride. I'm embarrassed by my desperation. By the need to chase down my brother while Eli can just hand over more than a thousand bucks anytime he wants.

I don't care what other people think about me, I remind myself.

I do my own thing. Take care of myself. Letting down my guard today totally screwed me.

I kick another rock.

What would a normal kid do right now, Hannah?

Forget normal. What would a reasonable kid do right now?

"She'd take the goddamn money," I say.

Because then she wouldn't get kicked out of her house, and that's far more important than pride.

So why aren't I doing it? Why aren't I being reasonable?

"Goddamn Eli. Goddamn Seth. Goddamn everyone."

Goddamn me *too.*

But maybe I know the answer to that too. It's not just that I don't want Eli to be an asshole. It's not just that he knows some of my secrets. It's that I *like* him. I really do.

Yeah, I still barely know him. But Eli's not pushy. He's been super helpful. He asked permission to kiss me, and he stuck around all night. Hell, he didn't even take off when the redhead's boyfriend was getting ready to kick his ass. Oh, and the way his lips feel helps a little too.

My face burns as I think about it. So much for not blushing, I guess.

Who would want to lose the chance to get closer to a guy like that? If I didn't like him, it wouldn't matter at all. I could grab the twelve hundred bucks and not feel bad. But taking money from him might change things. And that's the real reason I'm running away. Not my pride. Not because I can't see that paying the rent is more important. It's just because I like Eli, and I want the chance to like him even more.

I stop right where I am. I have to go back. I'm about to spin around when my phone buzzes in my pocket. I yank it out.

Unknown Caller, the screen reads.

Normally I wouldn't answer. But maybe I'm hoping it's Eli or something, because I tap the screen.

"Hello?" I say.

"Hannah." It's my brother.

I don't get a chance to say anything back to him before someone else speaks into the phone instead.

"Is this Hannah Dresher?" a rough voice asks. "Seth's sister?"

My whole body goes cold. "Yes. What's—"

"We have your brother. Bring a thousand dollars to the blue house on Welan Lane. Do it within an hour, or you'll both regret it."

And then the line goes dead.

Chapter Twelve

For the second time tonight, I run.

I need to get back to Eli before he takes off. The money I thought I couldn't take is now money I *have* to take. There's no choice.

In my head, I hear the threat again. *You'll both regret it.*

I'm not mad at Seth anymore. I'm too scared to be pissed off. What if I don't make the one-hour deadline? What if Eli's gone, or he's changed his mind about lending me the money?

I run faster.

The forest treetops appear above the roofs of the houses in front of me, and I'm thankful that I didn't get too far away. When I push my way around the final corner, I almost burst into tears. Eli is still there. Standing right where I left him, at the edge of the woods. He's staring down at his phone with a sad look on his face. Lips turned down. Shoulders hunched.

My fault, I think. *But I'll say sorry later.*

"Eli!" I call.

He lifts his head, his eyes widening when he spots me.

I don't slow down until I get all the way to him. Breathlessly I explain the phone call. Eli doesn't ask any questions. He doesn't make fun of me for freaking out. And he doesn't mock the fact that I had to come crawling back to him for help. Best of all, he doesn't make me ask for the money. He just hands over the envelope.

"Here," he says. "It's exactly a thousand bucks."

I still hesitate. I can't help it. How much more money does he have stuffed in his pockets? And how the hell is he not worried about getting jumped? Then again, maybe he's not used to being in places where that's likely. Being rich and all.

What's wrong with you, Hannah? None of that matters. Seth's life is on the line.

I breathe out and take the envelope from Eli. Then I fold it in half and shove the fat wad into my own pocket.

"Thank you," I say. "It might not be a big deal to you, but it is to me."

"Finding your brother is the most important thing," Eli replies.

"I'll pay you back," I add.

"I know." He pauses. "Do you want me to come with you?"

I want him to. Of course I want him to. But I shouldn't want that, and neither should he.

"You might get hurt, Eli," I say.

"Willing to risk it," he replies.

"Why?" The word bursts out like a bullet.

"I like you. I liked you the whole damn year, but I was too chickenshit to talk to you."

"Why?" I repeat.

I'm wasting precious minutes on selfish questions. But I have to know.

"Because you're awesome," Eli says with a shrug.

The statement should make me laugh my ass off, but it doesn't.

"How the hell am *I* awesome?" I ask.

"You give zero fucks what anyone thinks," he replies. "I admire that. I'm jealous of it. Also, I think you're pretty."

"I live in a shit box, and my life is a shit *show*," I tell him.

His mouth curves up. "But you don't disagree that you're pretty?"

"Shut up," I mutter. "You know what I mean. I can't afford to give any fucks. Because if I do, the gen pop at school will eat me alive. It's not something to be jealous of, trust me."

He gets serious again. "Why does it matter so much to you?"

"How could it not?" I counter.

"Are you saying you can't like me because I don't live in a shit box?"

"What? No."

"Then we're in agreement," Eli says. "I don't care what your life is like. I care about getting to know you. When I saw you standing outside that corner store tonight, I felt like it was fate."

"I don't believe in fate," I reply.

"No fate *or* magic? That's practically tragic. But I guess that's okay. Only one of us has to believe in those things. Happy to volunteer."

I stare at him. Eli means it. Every damn word.

"Fine," I say.

"Yeah?"

"I just said 'fine,' didn't I?"

"And you said we're heading for Welan Lane, right?" he replies. "I know a shortcut."

He grabs my hand like he's done it a gazillion times before, and he tugs me along.

For a minute or two, I feel okay. My worry over Seth is buried just under the surface, and the conversation with Eli feels like some weird breakthrough for me. My life sucks in a general way. That doesn't mean everything about it has to suck, though, does it? I can have some happy things.

But we get to Welan Lane quickly, and the fear comes rushing back in. I'm light-headed. My stomach is tossing itself around like a boat on the stormy ocean.

The blue house sticks out. Not just because of its color but because it's a lot older than the rest of the homes on the block. And the closer we get to it, the more out of place it seems. The fence is missing half its slats. The grass is overgrown with strangled weeds, and the windows are boarded up. On top of all that, the house is dark. Not a single bit of light escapes from anywhere that I can see.

Did the guy on the phone give me the wrong info? Is it some kind of trick?

Eli nudges my shoulder. "Look. The door's open."

I squint. He's right. The front door is moving back and forth with the evening breeze.

Still holding hands, we walk cautiously up the front pathway. The cement is crumbly under my feet. My skin is prickling. Everything about this seems like a bad idea, but I can't abandon my brother.

Besides which, the guys who have him threatened me too.

I pull my hand out of Eli's, and I give the door a push. I expect a noisy, rusty creak. But it opens in complete silence.

I step inside, and my breath catches in my throat.

Seth.

He's tied to a chair in the middle of the open living room. His body is limp, his head hanging down. And just above his eyebrow is a wicked cut, oozing fresh blood that's visible even in the dimness.

Chapter Thirteen

Seth is very, very still. Too still. And I'm equally frozen.

Please, no, I think. *Please, no.* Then faster, the same thought on repeat, moving in quick time with my heart. *Please-no, please-no, please-no.*

"Please no," I whisper.

Eli puts a hand on my elbow, and panic rises at the thought that he might drag me away. I yank free, able to move at last. I rush to Seth. And just as I reach him, he lets out a groan.

"Seth," I say. "It's me."

My brother's eyes are glassy, but they focus on me. "Hannah?"

His voice is a croak, but I'll take what I can get.

The tears I've been holding back all night burst through. An actual sob makes its way out of my throat too.

"My head hurts," Seth says.

"No shit," I reply.

"Who's that?" he asks, his glazed stare lifting over my shoulder.

I glance back. "That's Eli. And you can thank him for saving your ass as soon as we finish actually doing it."

"Hey, man," says Eli.

"Hey," Seth repeats.

My brother's head droops again after that, and my pulse jumps with nerves. I get to work untying him. It takes only a second, and thankfully, Seth seems a lot better when he can move. He rolls his shoulders. Groans again. Stands up. Sways for a moment. Then steadies himself using the back of the chair.

Eli gives me a nudge. "Look up to the ceiling on your left," he says softly.

I do. A blinking red light looks back at me. It's a camera. Held to its spot by a piece of duct tape. A detail that would make me roll my eyes under other circumstances. But not now. Right now it makes me shiver instead. They're watching us.

Slowly—deliberately—I pull the stuffed envelope from my pocket. I hold it up in clear view of the camera and open it to reveal the bills inside. And a heartbeat later my phone rings.

I don't bother to look at the screen before answering. "Hello?"

"Hello, Hannah Dresher," says the rough voice

from before. "You can put that money on the chair where your brother was."

I step over and do as instructed.

"Good girl," the voice says. "And now you have two minutes to get the hell out of here. Tell Seth not to fuck with us again."

The phone goes silent, and I stick it back in my pocket.

Hurry, hurry, says a little voice in my head.

Not that I need a reminder. My stomach is a rock, and my throat feels gross and thick. Like I can't breathe properly.

"Help me get him outside," I say to Eli.

He nods, and we each sling an arm around my brother's waist. We're lopsided because of Eli's height, and our shuffle to the door is awkward and a bit slow. But I don't care. I've never been so relieved to leave a place, and in my life, that's really saying something.

The air outside has gotten a lot colder in the last few minutes. Like a summer storm wants to get started. Wind pushes through my hair and throws it in my face, but I ignore it. The three of us keep going all the way to the end of the block.

Shuffle, shuffle, shuffle.

We turn the corner, and a car appears at the end of the road. My throat tightens even more. My skin tingles, and I expect the car to stop. Maybe have three or four guys jump out and go back on their word to let us go. But it doesn't happen. The car cruises by. I exhale. I want to move faster, but Seth is struggling.

"How much farther?" he asks, his voice still sounding scratchy and full of pain.

Eli answers him. "There's a playground pretty close by. We can rest there if Hannah thinks it's okay."

I nod. What else can I do? It's obvious that Seth needs a break.

The next few minutes are a crawl. A hobble instead of a shuffle. Two more cars pass us, and each time I ready myself for a fight that doesn't come. Finally we reach the park. The three of us sink down onto a bench, and none of us say a word for a long moment.

Eli is the one who speaks first. "I'll give you guys a minute."

He stands up and walks away without waiting for an answer. I watch him go. He's just out of earshot but not out of sight. And despite what I'd said to him about not wanting a bodyguard or a sidekick, I'm glad he's there.

Seth clears his throat. "So…who's Mr. Tall Guy?"

I want to be mad at the question. He's not the one who should be asking questions. But I'm not done being relieved that he's okay, so all I get is a bit annoyed.

"Really?" I reply.

He sighs. "I'm sorry, Hannah."

"Do you *want* to get us kicked out of the apartment?" I ask. "Did you *like* our last foster home?"

He looks down at his hands. His fingernails are dirty. His knuckles are definitely swollen, and I can't stop myself from picturing him in a fight that he lost in a big way.

When did it get this bad?

I swallow the lump in my throat.

"If it helps any, I did pay the rent," Seth says without looking up.

I blink. It's not what I expected to hear at all.

"Maybe you should tell me what happened," I say. "From the beginning."

He nods and opens his mouth. But before he can answer me, a raindrop flies down and smacks directly into his forehead. He wipes it off and looks up. By the time he drops his hand, the sky has already opened. In seconds the rain is pelting down. A full-force summer storm.

Eli hurries toward Seth and me. "Should we take this party inside somewhere?" he asks.

"Is it okay if we just go home?" Seth directs the question at me, and I nod.

But it's not until we help him up that I realize this will mean letting Eli get a look inside my life...in the realest way possible.

Chapter Fourteen

I'm not gonna lie. The idea that Eli is about to come with Seth and me into our apartment makes my stomach twist up. But it's not like I have a choice. Seth can't walk on his own, and I can't help him by myself either.

Kind of a metaphor for the whole night, isn't it?

I mean, there's a chance I might've saved Seth without Eli's help. I have no way of knowing. But what matters is that I'm glad I didn't have to. Such a weird feeling. For me, anyway. Hannah Dresher, accepter of help from a cute boy. *Really* weird.

Before too long we go around the corner that leads to our street, and our building is there in the middle of it. The gray cement looks worse than ever. A place slapped together for people who can't afford to complain about it.

Home sweet home.

But it *is* home, at least for now.

We go up the crumbling front steps. I use my shoulder to push open the glass door with the broken lock. We step past a bunch of discarded crap. Crumpled newspapers. An empty toolbox. A broken high chair. I don't apologize for it, even as I wonder what Eli's house looks like compared to this. Probably clean and tidy and full of nice things.

Yeah, well, he can leave if it bothers him, I think.

But somehow I know he won't care. He won't leave.

A warm feeling expands in my chest as we step inside the elevator.

"What floor?" Eli asks.

"Six," I tell him.

"Penthouse," Seth adds.

A few hours ago the joke would've made me want to die of embarrassment. We *are* on the top floor. But there's not even a chance of pretending it's nicer than the rest of the place. It's not funny. Except I'm smiling.

"Only the best for the Dreshers," I say.

Eli laughs, and Seth joins in as the doors close. The warm feeling gets even bigger. It's been a million years since I heard my brother laugh. I didn't even know how much I'd missed it until this second.

We get to our floor and step out. The paint on the walls is peeling. The carpet is so worn it looks like a mangy dog's back. I'm used to it. But it glares back at me in the current moment. Like it's daring me not to see how bad it is. Again, not gonna lie,

I'm self-conscious about it. But I keep my head high. Literally. My neck hurts from holding it so stiff.

"We're in six-oh-one," I say, and my voice doesn't even wobble.

We walk through the door into our apartment. Nothing has changed since I left. Why would it? The vodka bottle is right there. Its label is just as red. Just as loud.

Dysfunctional family alert, it seems to say. *Don't even try to forget it!*

But it's getting easier to let things slide off me. And Eli doesn't react to the mess either. And not in that way that people *pretend* they don't notice things.

He really doesn't care.

"Where do you want to be, bro?" he asks Seth.

The stiffness in my neck disappears.

"My room, if no one minds," says my brother.

We shift direction and head for the hall that leads to the bedrooms. My mom's door is closed, and Seth and I exchange a look. Maybe Mom's home, and maybe she's not. Maybe today will be the last day of this particular bender, and maybe it won't. I'm just glad I don't have to see her current boyfriend's naked body another time.

We keep going to our shared bedroom, where we push through my half. For the first time since we came into the apartment, Eli seems interested. Now I'm a bit nervous again. But this is different. This is about me, not about my life. Do we like the same bands? The same books? Does he like chicken nuggets as much as I do? Is it better to have more stuff in common or less?

"I owe you a grand," my brother says as we help him to his bed.

Eli shrugs. "Technically, you owe it to my parents. But they can afford it."

It isn't a brag. It's just a statement of fact. And I expect Seth to take the offer of basically free money. That's what he'd usually do. But he surprises me.

"I want to pay you—or them—back as soon as I can," Seth says. "I'll get a job or something."

Eli shrugs again. "My dad's property company is always looking for guys to do weekend work. I can hook you up when you're better."

"Sounds good," says my brother. "I really owe you."

"He really does," I add.

Eli stuffs his hands into his pockets. "No worries. I should get going. My parents have probably already called the cops or something."

"I'll walk you to the door," I reply.

It's a weirdly basic thing to say, given the night we've had. And to be honest, I wish he didn't have to leave. I want to ask him about the music and the books and the chicken nuggets. But I get why he has to go. And I need to finish sorting shit out with Seth anyway.

I grab his hand and pull him out of the room. We pause at the front door.

"Will you call me?" Eli asks.

"If you give me your number." I drag out my phone, unlock it and hand it to him.

He taps the screen. When he hands back the phone, I see that he's saved himself in my contacts as *Eli is awesome*.

"Nerd," I say to him.

He grins. "Call me."

"I will," I promise.

"Tomorrow," he suggests.

"Okay," I agree.

"Or later today. Since it's already kind of tomorrow."

"Later today," I repeat.

"See you, Hannah."

"See you, Eli."

He gives me a kiss. Not a quick one but not an urgent one. One that feels like he'll be able to do it again soon.

After he goes, I stay where I am for a few more seconds, just feeling good. Then I take a breath and head back up the hallway to talk to my brother.

Chapter Fifteen

Seth is lying on his bed with his eyes closed, and for a second I think he's asleep. I debate leaving him that way. We can deal with whatever we have to in the morning. It's not like our problems are going anywhere. Besides which, I'm so tired that my face hurts. And my brother is *actually* hurt and probably needs sleep even more than I do.

But when I start to go back to my side of the room, he clears his throat.

"I fucked up, Hannah." His voice is small and sad. "I really fucked up."

I sit on the end of his bed. "Tell me what happened."

Without opening his eyes, Seth explains how he borrowed some money a couple of months back. Not for anything big. A pair of shoes. Some weed. A jacket. Just a few hundred bucks. But the guys who hooked him up with the loan were shady.

What a surprise, I think, but I keep it to myself.

He tells me that they'd given him three months to pay up. But then they came back earlier than that to collect. And they wanted twice what they'd lent him. Also not a shock, in my mind. It seems Seth didn't expect it, though. When he didn't have the money, they gave him forty-eight hours. And when he couldn't pay up on time again, they tripled the debt. Demanded he find some way to get it to them before the end of the day.

"They followed me home and broke one of my fucking fingers." He lifts his hand, and I see the bad angle of his pinky. "And they smashed my phone too."

"You could've been killed or something, Seth," I say softly.

"I know." He meets my eyes. "Well. I know *now*."

I shake my head. "I don't understand why you'd take that kind of loan in the first place."

"I just get so…I dunno. Frustrated or whatever. Nothing ever goes our way."

I reach over and squeeze his arm. He sounds like he used to when we were little. Young. Confused. And so, so sad. It makes my chest burn.

"What would a normal kid have done?" I ask him.

The smallest smile tugs at my brother's mouth before falling away again. "The game doesn't help anymore, does it? We always have to go back to being *not* normal. I couldn't call the cops. I couldn't ask Mom, could I?"

I don't answer for a second. They're pretty much the exact same thoughts I had earlier tonight when I first started looking for him.

"You could've just asked me for help," I say. "What's more normal than making a mistake and asking your big sister to cover your ass?"

"Would you even have helped me?" he asks.

I open my mouth to tell him that of course I would've, but I snap my jaw shut again hella quick. Would I have listened about the loan-shark guys and been nice? Hard to say, if I'm being honest. I wouldn't have let him get kidnapped, obviously. But how mad would I have been? The lump in my throat is back.

"I'm sorry if I've been a shitty sister," I say. "I know I've been busy with work all summer."

"You're not a shitty sister," Seth replies. "Why do you think I paid the rent to our douchey landlord instead of to the dicks who broke my finger?"

I shake my head. "No clue."

"Because I figured no matter what they did to me, you and Mom shouldn't be out on your asses." He makes a face at me. "You and Mom when Mom is sober."

I don't want to laugh, but one bubbles up and escapes anyway. "Jesus Christ, Seth. That's awful."

"Kinda true, though."

We're both quiet for a minute.

"Tonight scared the hell out of me," Seth finally admits.

"Good," I say.

"Gee, thanks."

"You're my brother, and I love you, and I would rescue you from a hundred finger-breaking assholes. But I'd rather not have to, you know?"

"See? You're—" He lets out a yawn, then tries again. "You're a good sister."

I push to my feet. "I'll let you sleep. Do me a favor and try not to make any bad choices in your dreams."

"I'll do my best. Night, Hannah."

I ruffle his hair like he's five and head for the curtain between our spaces. I lift up the fabric, but I stop before I go through, and I turn back.

"Hey, Seth..." I say.

"Yeah?" He sounds as though he's half asleep already.

"We're our own kind of normal, okay?"

"Okay. But our normal sucks."

"Only if we let it suck," I reply.

I step into my half of the room and drop the curtain. I let out my own yawn. I barely have enough energy to get changed, but I make myself put on my pajamas before I flop down onto my bed. Right before I start to drift off, I pull out my phone and type a message to Eli.

Is it later yet?

I don't check to see if he answers. I know he will. I just pull the covers up to my chin, smile and close my eyes. Because for the first time in forever, I'm looking forward to waking up to my life.

Melinda Di Lorenzo has been writing professionally for more than a decade and is the author of *Counting Scars* and *Racing Hearts* in the Orca Soundings line. In 2013 she won Harlequin's annual So You Think You Can Write contest, which came with a publishing contract and launched her successfully into the romance world. Bullied as a teen, Melinda sought refuge in books. She now wants to provide that refuge for others, and she draws on her experience as the parent of three teens to craft stories that reflect modern struggles, without turning those struggles into stereotypes. She also supports young writers and makes an annual creative writing scholarship donation to École Salish Secondary. Melinda lives in Surrey, British Columbia.